For Isla and Lily – A.L.

For Katie, Benny, George and Maggie May – D.L.

First published in 2021 by Scholastic Children's Books
a division of Scholastic Ltd
Euston House, 24 Eversholt Street
London NW1 1DB

www.scholastic.co.uk

London – New York – Toronto – Sydney – Auckland
Mexico City – New Delhi – Hong Kong

Text copyright © Alex Latimer, 2021
Illustrations copyright © David Litchfield, 2021

HB ISBN 978 0702 30559 7
PB ISBN 978 1407 19368 7

All rights reserved
Printed in China

1 3 5 7 9 10 8 6 4 2

The moral rights of Alex Latimer and
David Litchfield have been asserted.

Papers used by Scholastic Children's Books are made
from wood grown in sustainable forests and other controlled sources.

Alex Latimer   David Litchfield

Pip & Egg

SCHOLASTIC

One bright afternoon, Pip met Egg.

They were both very happy to find a friend
who was the same size and shape.

Soon they saw each other every day.

"Pip," said Egg, "we are birds of a feather."
"Egg," said Pip, "we are two peas in a pod."

After a few weeks,
they pinky-promised
to be friends forever.

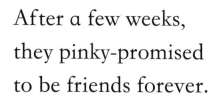

But then spring came, and something strange happened.

Pip began to grow a root –

and then a shoot!

Just like that, he found
himself planted in one spot.

He couldn't run or hop or swim with
his friend the way that he used to.

Luckily, it was a nice spot. He had a view down the valley to the river, and he was sheltered from the wind by a big rock.

Every day, Egg came by to visit Pip. They played I Spy and Rock-Leaf-Stick and all the other games they invented, while they watched the sky.

The weeks went by,

and Pip's shoot
became a proper stem

and on it grew a
few glossy leaves.

Then one day Egg arrived for her visit much later than usual. Pip heard a chirp from behind the big rock.

"Egg, is that you?" Pip asked.

In a way.

answered a small, sad voice.

When Egg stepped out, she was not the same Egg she'd been.

Now she had short wings, and a blue beak,
and scruffy feathers that looked like wet hair.

"I can't let anyone see
me like this," said Egg.

Pip understood.
"Stay here with me," he said.

So Egg stayed with Pip.

The days passed,
and they chatted

and told jokes

and made plans

– but then Egg's feathers began to grow longer and stronger.

She discovered that when she flapped her new wings they took her high into the air. She could see the whole landscape!

Her friend Pip and his valley became

a tiny speck.

When she got back, Egg panted, "Pip! I **have** to leave! There's a whole world to explore! I wish you could come."

"Me too," said Pip. "More than anything. But I have to stay here. You go, and come back soon. You know where I am."

Egg hugged Pip, and then
she took off into the air.

Pip reached up with his branches,
trying to follow her.

But he was rooted in the ground.
It felt to Pip that his heart had broken.

Egg flew over lakes and mountains and forests.
She saw glaciers, and beaches, and waterfalls pouring over cliffs.

She flew on until she came to
the most wonderful place of all

– the city!

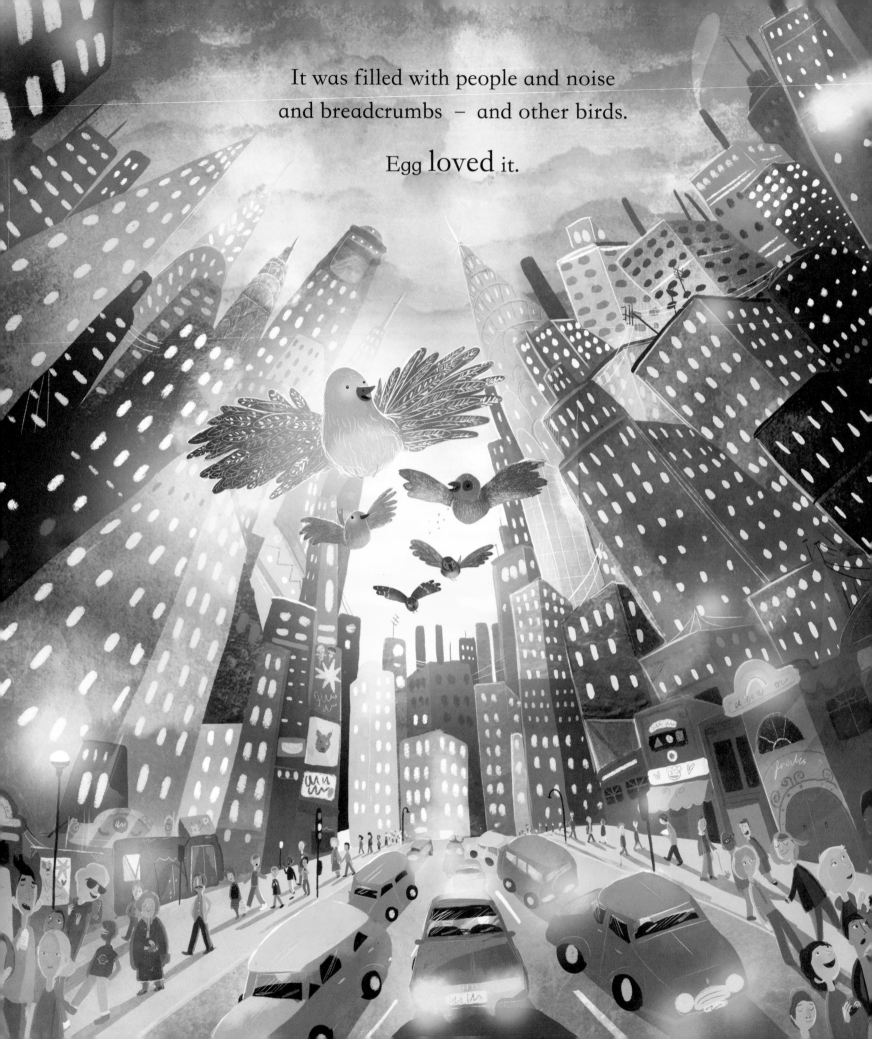

It was filled with people and noise
and breadcrumbs – and other birds.

Egg **loved** it.

She made friends.

She ate exciting foods.

She roosted on the
head of a statue.

Then, one morning, she felt something
new in her stomach: a big lump.

"You'll be a mother soon," said one of the
other birds. "You have an egg in there."

There was no one Egg wanted to tell more than her friend Pip.

And so she flew back to Pip, where he waited in his valley.

Egg knew exactly where to go.

Pip had grown into a sturdy
tree. His branches were
tipped with long green leaves
and bright white blossoms.

"Pip," called Egg, even before she'd landed. "I'm going to be a mother!"

Pip was very happy to see his old friend, and thrilled about her news. Egg told him everything. But then he spoke to her very seriously . . .

"Egg," said Pip. "Where will
you make your nest?
How will you choose out of all
the places in the world where
to lay your very own egg?"

Egg looked at Pip.

"It's true," she said, "I have seen so many wonderful places. But I have already decided on the best place in the world."

"Where is it?" asked Pip.

"Right here," said Egg. "I will build my nest in your very branches and lay my egg in this very spot, if you'll let me."

If he could have, Pip would have jumped for joy.

And so Egg built her home in Pip's branches, and gently set her egg in the nest.

Pip was careful not to sway too much in the wind.

They lived there side by side for the rest of their lives,
playing games and telling jokes and making plans.

They might even be there still.